King Keith is in ... ...s ...
Queen Freda insists on getting a lodger for the spare room.
The first person they see is Carmen de Screema – but she's too
noisy. The second person is The Amazing Flambo – but as a
fire-eater, he's too dangerous. Then a gust of wind blows the
door open and in walks Captain Roger Jolly, complete with
ear-ring, eye patch, cutlass, bushy red beard and shiny black
sea boots with silver buckles. The perfect lodger – a pirate!
Soon Roger becomes one of the family – everyone loves his
wonderful stories. Everyone, that is, except King Keith, and
he's in a bigger grump than ever. He sets out to get rid of the
jolly lodger and that's when the fun really starts.

Kaye Umansky has been a drama teacher, a TV presenter and a
singer in a band. She's now a full-time author. She has several
books in Puffin including *King Keith and the Nasty Case of
Dragonitus*, *Pongwiffy*, *Trash Hits* and *Witches in Stitches*. She
lives in London with her husband and young daughter.

Other books by Kaye Umansky

KAYE UMANSKY

KING KEITH
AND THE JOLLY
LODGER

ILLUSTRATED BY AINSLIE MACLEOD

PUFFIN BOOKS

PUFFIN BOOKS

Published by the Penguin Group
Penguin Books Ltd, 27 Wrights Lane, London W8 5TZ, England
Penguin Books USA Inc., 375 Hudson Street, New York, New York 10014, USA
Penguin Books Australia Ltd, Ringwood, Victoria, Australia
Penguin Books Canada Ltd, 10 Alcorn Avenue, Toronto, Ontario, Canada M4V 3B2
Penguin Books (NZ) Ltd, 182–190 Wairau Road, Auckland 10, New Zealand

Penguin Books Ltd, Registered Offices: Harmondsworth, Middlesex, England

First published by Viking 1991
Published in Puffin Books 1992
10 9 8 7 6 5 4 3

Printed in England by Clays Ltd, St Ives plc
Filmset in Linotron Palatino

Contents

No Gold

"Freda! Come down at once! I've got some terrible news!"

King Keith came panting up the stairs, crown askew.

"Have you, dearest? And what's that?" asked Queen Freda.

She was up a step-ladder repainting the ceiling of the spare room – the nice little turret room which overlooked the goldfish pond. For the first time in years, the palace was getting a face-lift.

"It's the gold! It's gone!" wailed King Keith. "I've just visited the treasury, and things are even worse than I thought. No

gold, plus we're half-way through the silver, and it's not even near the end of the month. We're going to have to stop spending. That means no more redecorating. I told you we couldn't afford that red carpet."

Queen Freda frowned and dipped her brush into the paint. She loved redecorating and certainly didn't intend to stop now. She was enjoying herself too much.

"Oh, really?" she said. "Well, that *is* a pity, because I've just ordered new curtains to match."

"Can't you send them back?" asked King Keith hopefully.

"I most certainly cannot," said Queen Freda firmly. "I've already torn up the old ones for dusters."

Just then, Princess Paula and Prince Percy came racing up the stairs. Both had their boots on, and there were muddy

footprints all over the stair-carpet.

"*Must* you wear those things indoors?" asked King Keith crossly. "No wonder everything in this palace wears out so quickly."

"What's the matter, Dad? You sound fed up," remarked Paula.

"The gold's gone," explained King Keith. "We're going to have to spend less. Tighten our belts. Keep costs down. Pinch, scrape and look after the pennies. Recycle,

reuse, save, make do, hoard, waste
nothing. Starting now."

"It's pocket-money day today," Percy
reminded him. "Does that mean we don't
get any?"

"Certainly you shall have your pocket
money, dear," promised Queen Freda.
"Daddy will find a way. Won't you, Keith?"

"Actually, right now I can't think of
one," confessed King Keith.

Just then, the Lord Chamberlain came

hurrying up, looking worried. Hot on his heels came Doctor Coldfingers, the royal doctor. They had just heard the news from Cook, who always seemed to know these things.

"Cook says the gold's gone!" they gasped. "Is it true, Your Majesty? Are things really that bad?"

"Worse," King Keith corrected them. "The Queen has spent most of the remaining silver on wallpaper. So we can forget the holiday this year. No more doughnuts on Saturdays or trips to the circus. No new clothes. No toys or sweets or treats. No more pay rises or pocket money. No more paint, paper, carpets or curtains."

There was a united groan. Everyone looked at each other with long faces. All except Queen Freda, who was made of sterner stuff.

"Nonsense," said Queen Freda briskly.

"If the gold's gone, we'll just have to earn some more. We must take on extra jobs."

There was an even louder groan. Everybody thought they worked quite hard enough as it was.

"There must be another way," pondered the Lord Chamberlain. "Why don't we all go away and think about it and meet at the kitchen table in one hour?"

And that's just what they did. Everyone went away to their private thinking places and racked their brains. One hour later, they met up in the kitchen and shared ideas over mugs of cocoa and slices of Cook's chocolate cake.

"Order!" called King Keith, and rapped the table with the sugar spoon. "Right, let's have your ideas. Youngest first. Off you go, Paula."

"We put on a show," said Paula, who had just started dancing classes, "and charge the loyal subjects to come and

watch. The Lord Chamberlain can play his recorder. You and Mum can sing a song or something. I don't know about the doctor, maybe he can work the curtains or sell ice-cream. I'll do a dance, of course."

"Hmm," said King Keith doubtfully. "I don't think we can expect the loyal subjects to *pay* to listen to the Lord Chamberlain playing his recorder. No need to look so hurt, Lord Chamberlain, you know you're terrible. How about you, Percy? What's your idea?"

"Rob a bank," said Percy, who could be silly sometimes.

"He's practising to be a comedian," explained Paula. "For my show."

King Keith ignored them both and turned back to the Lord Chamberlain.

"What about you, Lord Chamberlain? Do you have a suggestion?"

"Well, I had a word with my Aunty Vera, and she suggested something called

a Bring and Buy Sale . . ." said the Lord
Chamberlain, sounding vague. "I think we
bring things and buy them back. I don't
quite understand how it works, but it's
supposed to make money."

King Keith didn't look convinced.

"Borrow some," said Doctor Coldfingers
firmly. "That's my prescription. Find some
people with pots of money and invite them
to tea. Then borrow some. I can't see any
other way."

"Well, I can," said Queen Freda.
Everyone sat up and paid attention,
because Queen Freda usually had sensible
ideas. "We'll take a lodger. We now have a
beautifully decorated spare room, so we'll
advertise for someone to come and live in
it. I've already written out the advertisement.
Percy and Paula, you can take it to the post
office and stick it in the window."

Everyone stared admiringly at Queen
Freda's card. Everyone except King Keith.

He stared at it with horror. It was very neat, and it said:

Lodger Wanted
Quiet, safe, friendly lodger
required for spare room at
palace. Bed, breakfast and
evening meal provided.
Ten gold pieces per week.
Apply Queen Freda

"There are sure to be hundreds of applicants," said Queen Freda confidently. "We'll have to interview them, of course. We'll form a proper interviewing panel, so that everybody has a fair say."

"Congratulations, Queen Freda," said the Lord Chamberlain. "What a brilliant idea. Let's give that one a little clap, shall we?"

And everyone agreed. Everyone except King Keith.

"What's the matter, dearest?" asked

Queen Freda. "I see you're not clapping."

"I don't want a lodger," said King Keith.

"Not even a quiet, safe, friendly one?" coaxed Doctor Coldfingers.

"No," said King Keith. "I don't want strangers coming into my palace. They'll get in the way. I think it's a terrible idea."

"Oh, really?" said Queen Freda.

"What's *your* money-making idea then?"

But King Keith hadn't thought of one.

"Oh well," said Queen Freda rather huffily. "That's that, then. No lodger, no gold. I'll just tell Cook to cancel the doughnuts for tea. We'll have bread and water instead."

"On second thoughts," said King Keith, "I suppose we should give it a try."

"That's settled then," said Queen Freda.

Quiet, Safe and Friendly

"Well? How many hundreds of quiet, safe, friendly people do we have to see, Mum?" asked Prince Percy eagerly. It was the following day and the interviewing panel was assembled in the throne room. The panel consisted of King Keith, Queen Freda, Percy, Paula, the Lord Chamberlain, Doctor Coldfingers and the cat. Cook had been asked, but couldn't spare the time.

"Two," said Queen Freda, consulting her list.

"Two *hundred*?" gasped the interviewing panel.

"No, two," repeated Queen Freda. "It was rather a disappointing response. Never mind, I'm quite sure one of them will be suitable. The first is called Senorita Carmen de Screema. She's an opera singer. Doctor Coldfingers, be a dear and ask her to step in, would you?"

"I don't want an opera singer," objected King Keith. He had spent a terrible night tossing and turning in the grip of terrifying nightmares, all of which featured lodgers. Lodgers who took liberties. Cheeky lodgers who sat on his throne. Spooky lodgers who sleepwalked. Noisy lodgers who played the trumpet. Greedy lodgers who took the biggest roast potato *and the last piece of pie*!

"In fact," added King Keith, "in fact, I've definitely decided I don't want a lodger. I've changed my mind."

But he was too late, because the doors crashed open and in swept Carmen de

Screema. She was very big. She wore a
huge hat dripping with fruit and feathers
and lots of jewellery. She had long curly
red hair and matching fingernails. She
spoke in a booming voice and waved her
hands around a lot when she talked. Percy
and Paula nudged each other and giggled.

"'Allo, darleengs," said Carmen de
Screema. "You wanna lodger? Looka no
more. I am Carmen de Screema, the

famous opera star. I needa leedle corner to practeese my seenging."

"Do you practise a lot?" enquired Queen Freda politely.

"Alla the day and alla the night," explained Carmen de Screema. "I am an artiste. I only 'appy eef I seeng. You wan' I seeng for you now? Leesten. I perform for you my 'ighest note."

Carmen de Screema took a deep breath

and let out a high-pitched screech. The cat on Paula's lap leaped for the window with a hiss. Queen Freda's best flower vase cracked into a thousand pieces. Several miles away, a dog started barking.

"You wanna another?" asked Carmen de Screema. "I theenk I can go 'igher."

"No thank you," said King Keith hastily. His ears were ringing, and he felt a headache coming on. "We'll let you know."

Carmen de Screema looked offended.

"Suita youselfa," she said, and flounced out.

"No opera singers," said King Keith. "Too noisy. Who's next?"

"I must admit I'm a little worried about this one myself," confessed Queen Freda. "The Amazing Flambo. I believe he's a fire-eater with the circus. He doesn't sound very suitable."

"Oh, Mum! Please!" begged Percy and

Paula, who thought The Amazing Flambo sounded perfect.

"Think of the curtains," fretted Queen Freda.

"But it wouldn't be fair to send him away without even *seeing* him," said the Lord Chamberlain slyly. He knew Queen Freda always liked to be fair.

"I agree," said Doctor Coldfingers, who loved the circus. "We should give him a chance."

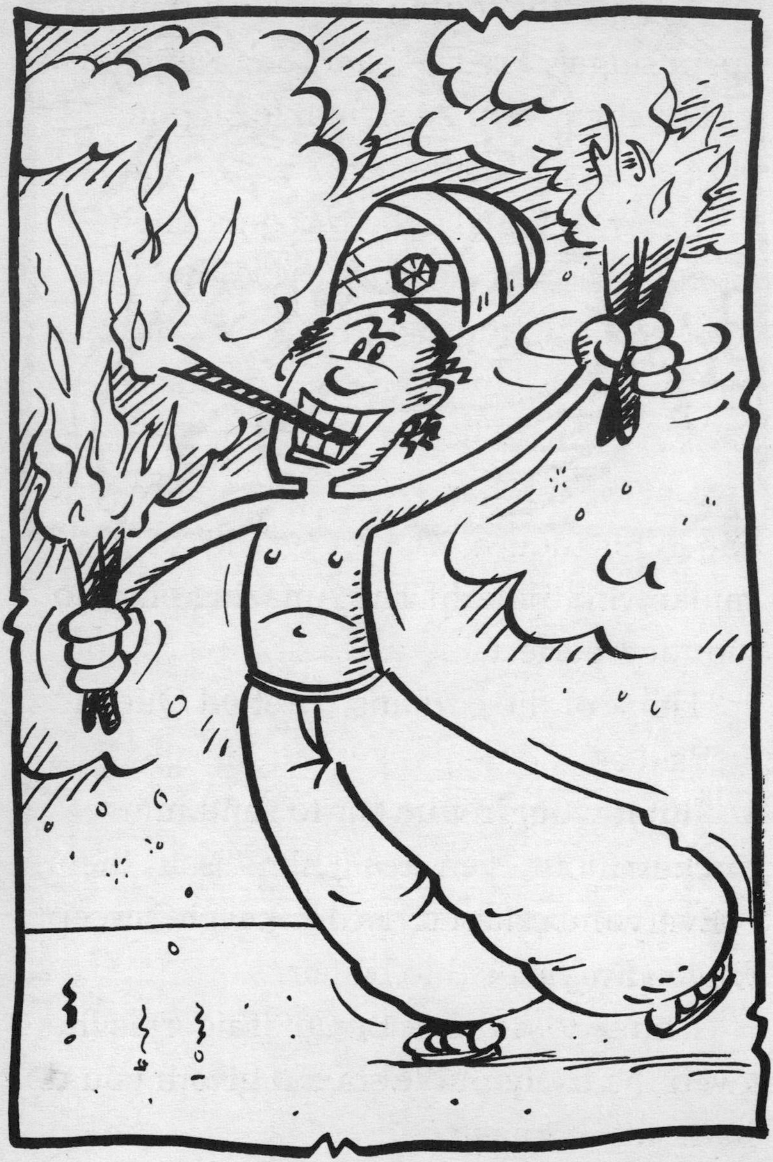

"A fire-eater couldn't be worse than an opera singer, Freda," said King Keith, also a keen circus fan. "Ask him to step in, please, Lord Chamberlain."

The Amazing Flambo certainly knew how to make an entrance. He came somersaulting through the door wearing a turban and baggy trousers. To Queen Freda's dismay, he held *five burning torches*! Two in the left hand, two in the right, and one in his mouth. There was a lot of smoke, and little sparks kept dropping on the carpet. He came to a halt, bowed and spoke.

"Ladies and gents, for your delight I shall now juggle with these flaming torches!"

Everyone clapped encouragingly, except Queen Freda.

"You'll do no such thing," said Queen Freda. "Kindly put them out before you do some real damage."

The Amazing Flambo looked disappointed. One by one, he stuck the burning clubs into his mouth. Each time he did so, there was a small sizzling noise and the flame went out. At the same time, Queen Freda gave a little shudder.

"I've come about the room," explained The Amazing Flambo, once he was no longer a fire risk. "I saw your advertisement in the post office. I just

thought you might like to see my act. I
can get free tickets for the circus, if
anyone – ?''

''Me! I'll have one!'' quickly chorused
King Keith, Percy, Paula, the Lord
Chamberlain and Doctor Coldfingers. But
Queen Freda kept her head.

''I'm sure you are talented, Mr Flambo,''
she said in a businesslike way. ''But are
you *safe*?''

"Definitely," nodded The Amazing Flambo, stamping on the smouldering carpet. "Oops, sorry, didn't see that one."

"And why do you wish to lodge with us here at the palace?"

"My caravan caught fire," explained The Amazing Flambo.

"We'll let you know," said Queen Freda firmly.

"Oh dear," said Queen Freda with a sigh. "How disappointing. You would have thought that *one* of them would have been right, wouldn't you?"

"I told you," crowed King Keith. "What did I say? I said it was a terrible idea. Perhaps next time you'll all pay a bit of attention to me."

"There's no need to sound so smug, Keith," said Queen Freda sharply. "We still haven't solved the gold problem, remember? Unless you have a fairy godmother up your sleeve that we don't know about."

"My goodness, look how dark it's getting," said King Keith. "It must be nearly tea-time. And, do you notice? There's quite a wind blowing up."

He was right. As he spoke, the throne-room door rattled, and a sudden squall of rain spattered the windows. Queen Freda got up and pulled the curtains. The Lord Chamberlain lit the lamps.

"I can smell something funny," said Paula suddenly. "What is it?"

"It smells like the seaside," said Percy. "Sort of clean and salty."

"Ssh," said Doctor Coldfingers. "Footsteps."

Everyone listened. Sure enough, heavy footsteps were approaching.

"It's that Carmen de Screema woman coming back," said King Keith nervously.

"It's Cook coming to tell us tea is ready," said Doctor Coldfingers hopefully.

"Perhaps it's Daddy's fairy godmother," said Paula with a giggle.

"Nonsense, it'll be Mr Flambo," said Queen Freda. "Come in, Mr Flambo. I'm afraid we have decided not to let . . . let . . ."

The door swung open and Queen Freda trailed to a halt. For the person standing in the doorway was not The Amazing Flambo. Oh dear me, no.

Roger

"It's a pirate!" gasped Percy and Paula.

And it was.

The man in the doorway simply couldn't have been anything else. He had the lot. He had the ear-ring, the eye patch, the bushy red beard, the long purple coat trimmed with gold braid, the three-cornered hat, the sharp cutlass, the silver pistol and the shiny black sea boots with silver buckles. A bottle of rum peeped from his pocket. He even had a parrot on his shoulder. It was a damp, green, cross-looking one with beady eyes. The only thing he didn't have was a wooden leg.

"Ahoy there, mateys," boomed the pirate – which is, of course, exactly what he should have said. And he said it in sort of a sea-deep rumble with an inbuilt chuckle that made everyone except King Keith like him immediately.

"Ahoy there!" chorused Percy and Paula enthusiastically.

"I say!" muttered the Lord Chamberlain, terribly impressed.

"He's got the wrong palace," whispered Doctor Coldfingers. "He must have."

King Keith was suffering from an acute case of instant dislike, and didn't say anything.

"Please come in, Mr er . . .?" invited Queen Freda, remembering her manners.

The pirate strode forward, took Queen Freda's hand and bowed deeply.

"I thankee, Yer Majesty. I've left me sea-chest outside. Don't want it drippin' all over yer nice carpets. 'Tis a wild night out."

"It wasn't until you arrived," remarked King Keith, finding his voice.

"No? Aye, well, likely you'm right. Storms got a way o' following me an' Pamela about. Ain't that right, Pamela?"

The cross, wet parrot on his shoulder rudely turned her back and refused to say a thing.

"How can we help you, Mr – er?" asked Queen Freda.

"Jolly's the name, lovely lady," said the pirate. "Cap'n Roger Jolly o' the Naughty Norma at your service, and this 'ere's Pamela. Just back from the Pinacoladas and takin' a spot o' shore leave while the crew unloads the pineapples. Me first proper 'oliday in years, matter o' fact. First chance I've had to get the salt out o' me lungs and spend some o' me hard-earned gold. I heard you got a room to let."

"I don't think you're on my list," said Queen Freda, getting all pink and

flustered. She wasn't used to being called lovely lady.

"No, marm," agreed Cap'n Roger Jolly. "Us seafaring men of action don't hold with lists. When you'm sailing into a force ten gale, it's amazin' 'ow you can never find a pencil."

And he threw back his head and bellowed with hearty laughter. The Lord Chamberlain, Doctor Coldfingers and Percy and Paula joined in. So did Queen Freda. King Keith and the parrot didn't.

"I thought sailors stayed in inns," remarked King Keith. "I thought it was traditional."

"Well, normally we do. But what I says is, why stay in an inn when you can stay in a palace?"

Still chortling, Cap'n Roger Jolly turned to Queen Freda and treated her to another of his swashbuckling bows. He then

withdrew a chinking cloth bag from one of
his deep pockets.

"Marm," he said. "This old sea dog's
walked a fair mile this night, and has a
mind to get his boots off. Beggin' yer
leave, we'll discuss details in the morning.
In the mean time, 'ere's a bag o'gold to be
startin' with. Me first week's rent, in
advance. Look lively, then, young
shipmates. Will ye give the cap'n a hand

with the luggage and show him to his cabin?''

He gave Percy and Paula a friendly wink.

''Oh yes, Mum, yes!'' begged Percy and Paula. ''Can we? Can we?''

''I'll handle this, Freda,'' said King Keith. ''Look, Mr – er – Captain Jolly, I'm afraid . . .''

''Call me Roger,'' said the pirate. ''Roger the lodger, eh? Ha, ha, ha!''

And he burst into such loud, jolly guffaws of laughter that everyone except King Keith felt they simply *had* to join in. And the more they laughed, the more they wanted to laugh.

"Roger the lodger," chuckled Doctor Coldfingers, wiping his eyes. "That's a good one, that is."

"I'm afraid it's out of the question," said King Keith stiffly. "I've just remembered

that someone is coming to stay. The spare room isn't spare any more. Goodnight. Thank you for coming. Try the Pig and Slopbucket, straight out the gate and turn left, you can't miss it."

There was an awkward silence. Roger looked at King Keith and shook his head.

"What's up, shipmate?" he asked sadly. "Be it the way I look? Or my plain manner o' speech? Be it the beard? Don't ye trust me?"

"Of course he does," said Queen Freda, Percy, Paula, the Lord Chamberlain and Doctor Coldfingers soothingly.

"But . . . Freda! You wrote the advertisement! You wanted someone quiet, safe and friendly!" hissed King Keith. "Those were your very words."

"Oh, do be quiet, Keith," said Queen Freda briskly. "I'm sure Captain Jolly is just the sort of person we're looking for. Anyway, I wouldn't dream of turning him

out on a wild night like this. Welcome to
our little palace, Captain. Make yourself at
home."

"Roger," said Roger, with a deep
chuckle. "Roger the lodger. Remember?"

"Roger," said Queen Freda.

The Jolly Lodger

"Two hours! Two hours he's been in the bathroom!" seethed King Keith.

"Do calm down, Keith," said Queen Freda. "What do you think? Shall I wear this one, or the one with the rubies?"

It was the following morning. Queen Freda was sitting at her dressing-table trying on crowns whilst King Keith strode to and fro in his bathrobe and flicked at things with his towel.

"He's a pirate, I tell you!" insisted King Keith. "He's doing replays of old pirate battles in the bath with toy boats, I heard him. He's got a tattoo! An anchor on his

right hand, you must have seen it. He
sings songs about walking the plank! Last
night he was drinking rum in his bedroom,
I could smell it. He's using my bubble
bath! How much evidence do you need? A
pirate in a palace – it's just not right.
You've got to get rid of him, Freda."

"Don't be ridiculous," said Queen
Freda. "Roger is not a pirate. He is a sea
captain. There is a great difference. I don't

want to hear another word."

King Keith threw himself into a chair and moped. He had been waiting to use the bathroom for two whole hours while Roger splashed and ran hot water and bellowed sea shanties and helped himself to King Keith's talcum powder.

Keith wanted to rattle the knob and shout to Roger to come out, but Queen Freda wouldn't let him. She said that

everyone deserves a good, long soak from time to time, especially if you'd been at sea.

"Stop fussing and have your bath after breakfast," suggested Queen Freda. "After all, that's when you usually have it."

Even breakfast didn't help matters much. As well as the usual things, King Keith noticed that Cook had one or two new items on the menu.

"Kippers? Rum? We've never had those for breakfast before," he complained to Queen Freda, Princess Paula, Prince Percy, the Lord Chamberlain and Doctor Coldfingers. "How come Roger gets them?"

"Because Cook wants him to feel at home, of course," explained Queen Freda.

"I think he feels that all right," said Percy. "He's put the bed out on the landing. Paula and I helped him. He says he prefers to sleep in a hammock. He

showed us how to sling it. Can I sleep in a hammock, Mum?"

"Certainly not," said Queen Freda.

"What else did you see?" asked the Lord Chamberlain, Doctor Coldfingers and King Keith curiously.

"Well," began Paula. "He's got a concertina and a telescope."

"And he sleeps with his cutlass at the ready," said Percy.

"And Pamela snores," continued Paula. "And he's put charts on the wall. And he's going to teach us knots, and show us how to build a crow's-nest. And make a special drink with raisins and rum."

Just at that moment Roger came into the kitchen. He was wearing a clean frilly white shirt and a fresh eye patch. His red beard was neatly combed and his boots and buttons shone brightly. He smelled strongly of King Keith's rose-scented talcum powder. Pamela sat on his shoulder and glared through beady little eyes.

"Morning, mateys," boomed Roger. "And a fine one it is to be sure."

"Oh good," said King Keith sourly. "You're out of the bathroom, then."

"Aye. Nothing like a good, long soak. Especially when you've been at sea."

From behind his back, Roger brought a red rose, which he presented to Queen Freda with a bow.

"Nipped out and cut it from the garden myself," he explained.

"That's off my prize rose bush!" gasped King Keith, horrified.

"Only the best for such a lovely lady," said Roger, with a wink to Percy and Paula.

"Thank you, Roger," said Queen Freda, glaring at King Keith. "It was a very nice thought."

"Do sit down, Captain," invited Doctor Coldfingers, jumping to his feet and brushing off a chair with his handkerchief.

"Roger," said Roger with a wink.

"Roger, over and out," said Doctor Coldfingers, which was quite funny for him.

"Did you sleep well, Roger?" enquired the Lord Chamberlain.

"Aye, thankee – though I missed the sea slappin' outside the porthole and the creakin' o' the timbers and the cries o' the watch. Talkin' o' timbers reminds me o' somethin' funny. I were a cabin boy at the time, couldn't have been more than seven or thereabouts. We was bound for the Isle of Allspice, I remember, and the captain's name was Timbertoes. There was this carpenter called Boss-Eyed Benny . . ."

And Roger began to tell a story. It was a funny story, and he was a wonderful story-teller. He did all the actions and all the voices. At one point, he did a hornpipe

on the table. A bit later on in the story, he mimed Boss-Eyed Benny trying to hammer a nail. By the end of it, everyone except King Keith was in fits. Queen Freda was wiping her eyes with her hanky. Percy and Paula's ribs ached, and the Lord Chamberlain and Doctor Coldfingers were sobbing on each other's shoulders.

But King Keith was sulking and didn't crack his face.

"Roger Jolly," he said coldly. "That's an unusual name. Turn it the other way round, of course, and you get Jolly Roger. Isn't that the name for the p– ?"

"Tea or coffee, Roger?" asked Queen Freda.

"Here, Roger. Have the paper," said Doctor Coldfingers.

"Do have the menu, Roger," said the Lord Chamberlain, passing it. "I'm sure

you sailors have hearty appetites.''

"That we do,'' agreed Roger, studying the menu. "And talking of appetites reminds me o' the famous pie-eating contest between Big Boris, cap'n o' the Greedy Glenda, and Peg Leg Pete, terror o' the seven seas . . .''

"Excuse me,'' said King Keith. "I think I'll take the dog for a walk. Does anyone want to come?''

But nobody did. Everyone wanted to hear about the pie-eating contest.

So King Keith walked the dog on his own.

King Keith's Blues

From that moment on, King Keith did a lot
of lonely dog walking. He would sit on
chilly hillocks and sulkily stare back at the
distant palace. The dog would wag its tail
and lick his face, hoping that he might
throw a stick. But he never did.

Back at the palace, everybody else was
having loads of fun – and all because of
Roger. He carved Percy and Paula a whole
fleet of sailing ships and helped sail them
on the pond. He built them a proper
crow's-nest in the highest tree in the
garden. He showed the Lord Chamberlain
how to put a ship in a bottle and gave

concertina lessons to Doctor Coldfingers.
He took the pair of them down to the Pig
and Slopbucket to help him spend his
hard-earned gold. He loaned Pamela to
Cook, who had taken to her, and promised
to pass on the secret of making a good
nourishing fish dip. He loaned Queen
Freda his telescope and promised to show
her the stars. He organized fishing trips
and community shanty singing. Everybody

agreed that Roger was indeed the perfect lodger.

Everybody except King Keith, that is. Keith didn't like him.

"I don't like him," he told the dog. "I never wanted a lodger in the first place. But I most especially didn't want him."

The dog opened one eye and licked his hand dutifully.

"I don't like him," he grumbled to the

Lord Chamberlain. "He's a pirate. Pirates are thieves and cut-throats. We'll be robbed in our beds."

"Oh, really, Your Majesty," said the Lord Chamberlain. "I think you're being just a tiny bit unfair, don't you? Why would he rob us? He's the one with the gold, remember? We haven't got any. Look, I can't stop and talk now. It's time for my hornpipe lesson."

"I don't like him," King Keith confided to Doctor Coldfingers. "He's dangerous. I think he might be a health risk."

But Doctor Coldfingers was practising the concertina and didn't even hear.

"I don't like him," King Keith announced to Percy and Paula. "He's putting ideas into your heads. You're even beginning to talk like him. Soon you'll be running away to become cabin boys."

"Cabin *girl* if ye don't mind, by thunder," Paula corrected him. "Come on,

Percy lad. Let's go and pack our kits before the tide turns."

"I'm not saying I don't *like* him," said King Keith carefully to Queen Freda. "It's just that I think I'm allergic to Pamela. Achoo!"

"Do be quiet, Keith, and pass up the paste bucket," said Queen Freda. She was papering the loft and didn't want to be bothered. Since Roger had started paying his ten gold pieces, she was back redecorating and loving every minute.

"I just don't like him," repeated King Keith to the dog. "But nobody will hear a word against him. Things are changing, Monty. Nobody pays any attention to *me* any more. They're all too busy with Roger. Roger this, Roger that. I tell you, it's beginning to get me down."

But when he looked down, the dog had gone. For a walk. With Roger.

"That's it," said King Keith. "Even the

dog's on his side. Roger has got to go."

But how to make him? That was the trouble. King Keith couldn't go too far because Queen Freda wouldn't let him. So he was mean and petty in silly little ways.

He took to getting up at the crack of dawn, to try and beat Roger to the bathroom.

He bought a large padlock for the cupboard where he kept his bubble bath

and talcum powder and painted KEEP
OUT! PROPERTY OF THE CROWN
in stern black letters on the door.

He refused to come in for meals.
Instead, he took cheese sandwiches down
to the potting shed and ate them on his
own.

He refused to join in the community
shanty singing.

He coughed and rustled *The Royal Times*

when Roger told one of his stories.

Queen Freda, Percy, Paula, the Lord Chamberlain and Doctor Coldfingers were truly exasperated.

"Oh, really, Keith!" scolded Queen Freda. "You're being such a baby. I do believe you're jealous!"

"Me? Jealous? Of a pirate? Me? Hah!"

"He might be a pirate, but he's better behaved than you are," remarked Queen Freda. "Also, he keeps his room shipshape and pays his rent on time."

It was true. King Keith was behaving extremely badly. Roger noticed it, of course. He took to clapping King Keith on the back and saying things like "Cheer up, matey," and "'Tis only a storm in a teacup". In fact, he went out of his way to be friendly. He insisted on lending King Keith his cutlass. He offered to show him a new knot.

Nothing helped. The nicer he was, the

more King Keith disliked him. He really
had a bee in his crown. The trouble was,
Roger showed no signs of leaving. So,
what to do? Snoop, that was what. Snoop
and get some hard evidence.

Snooping

King Keith stealthily opened the door of
the spare room. He glanced nervously over
his shoulder before scuttling in and closing
the door behind him. It wouldn't do to be
caught. He could imagine what Queen
Freda would say. He had a story prepared
about hearing a mysterious noise, but he
didn't think it would hold up.

Curious, he stared around. Percy and
Paula were right. It was just like a ship's
cabin.

A stiff breeze blew in from the open
window and set the hammock swinging.
Lots of complicated-looking nautical

instruments hung on the wall together with a painting of the Naughty Norma done on velvet. There were charts, maps, an ancient globe, a stuffed fish, coiled ropes, a collection of driftwood and a bucket of rather smelly seaweed. There was an opened packet of parrot seed. There was Roger's concertina. There was also a large framed photograph of a pipe-smoking lady in a spotted headscarf. Scrawled across it were the words "From your Ma" followed by lots of kisses.

There was, too, a large, battered old sea-chest. It was this that caught King Keith's eye. It looked as though it held secrets. Perhaps treasure maps, or private postcards?

Holding his breath, he ran on tiptoe to the sea-chest. Wonder of wonders, it wasn't locked! The old hinges squealed slightly as King Keith raised the lid and peered in.

And this is what he saw:

Bags of gold. Bejewelled pistols and cutlasses. A change of socks. Strings of pearls. Diamond rings and brooches. A thick, tattered book entitled *Practical Pirating*. Underpants. And right at the bottom lay a neatly folded black flag bearing the emblem of the *skull and crossbones*! Even better, lying between the flag's folds lay . . . the Naughty Norma's log-book!

King Keith reached in, picked up the log-book and opened it. It was written in bold black handwriting, and this is what it said:

Captain Roger Jolly. Ship's Log
Last Week at Sea.

Monday: Last night dreamed about my holiday. Got up, porridge for breakfast. Stiff northwesterly today. Sunk ship. Loads of booty, mostly gold.

Tuesday: Can't wait for holiday.
    Roll on end of voyage. Mean-
    while business as usual. Got
    up, porridge for breakfast.
    Sunk another ship. More
    booty. Rubies, sapphires,
    gold, the usual

Wednesday: Only three more days
    to go. Got up, porridge for
    breakfast. Put down a
    mutiny. Sunk two more
    ships. Is this a record?

And so on.

This was it! All the proof he needed.

Triumphantly, King Keith stuffed the
log-book down the front of his robe and
reached out for the folded pirate flag,
which was his other main piece of
evidence. That's when he heard a sound –
or, rather, two sounds.

73

The first was footsteps coming up the
stairs. The second was Roger's cheery
voice singing.

"A tender heart has fearsome Frank
He'll grant you two last wishes,
He'll let you walk upon his plank
Before you feed the fishes . . ."

What happened next happened so
quickly that everything got tangled up in a
blur of action. Here it is slowed down:

King Keith panicked and jerked back
from the chest, dropping the lid on his
finger . . . He staggered to his feet and the
neatly folded Jolly Roger unfurled and
flowed down to the floor . . . King Keith
tripped over the hem and landed painfully
on his knees . . . There now followed a brief
wrestling match on the floor between Keith
and the flag. The flag won by winding
itself round his head . . . King Keith
stumbled to his feet and tried to rid himself

of the annoying thing which seemed intent on strangling him. In doing so, he knocked over the bucket of seaweed . . . At this point, Roger entered the room at a run. He took one look at the sinister figure who appeared to be attempting to disguise itself in the pirate flag. "Ahar!" roared Roger, brandishing his sword and pistol. "So 'tis a thief, is it? Stop, thief, in the name of the King, or you'm dead as bilge-water!" At the same moment, Pamela rose from his shoulder and launched a mid-air attack on King Keith, who tottered, backed away, lost his balance on the slippery floor and went into a flailing, backwards run . . . which ended in a surprisingly neat backwards somersault straight out of the open window!

The spare room was high up in a turret. It could have been serious.

But it wasn't.

Very, very luckily for King Keith, he was

still wrapped in the Jolly Roger. It was that which saved him. It billowed out, slowing him down, acting as a sort of parachute.

Then, amazingly, the flag caught on a stone which was jutting out some way below the window ledge. There was a slight tearing sound, which, thankfully, soon stopped. King Keith and the turret wall came together in a sort of unpleasant

smack – and finally, King Keith just swung. And clung.

And held his breath.

And closed his eyes.

And tried not to look down.

Reeled In

Far below, the Lord Chamberlain and Doctor Coldfingers were taking a stroll in the garden. They were testing each other on parts of a sailing ship.

"Mizen-mast," said Doctor Coldfingers. "Rudder. Poop deck . . ."

"Listen," said the Lord Chamberlain.

"Oh yes, of course. Almost forgot that. Poop deck. Lisson . . ."

"No, I mean *listen*. Do you hear a feeble cry?"

"I believe I do," agreed Doctor Coldfingers. And they both looked up.

"It's the King," observed the Lord

Chamberlain. "Dangling."

"Bless my stethoscope, you're right," gasped Doctor Coldfingers.

At exactly the same moment, Queen Freda, Percy, Paula and the dog arrived back from the shops. The dog pulled the lead out of Queen Freda's hand and raced to the foot of the tower from which King Keith dangled helplessly. Once there, it barked excitedly.

"It's Daddy!" shouted Paula. "He's fallen out of Roger's window!"

"Quick, let's get a tablecloth from the washing line!" yelled Percy. "We can hold it out for him to fall into."

And they both ran off.

"The things he does to draw attention to himself," sighed Queen Freda.

"Help!" cried King Keith. "I'm slipping. Somebody fetch a ladder or something."

Just then, a voice spoke from high above his head.

"Hold on, matey," said Roger's cheery voice. And his big red beard appeared in the window. Pamela had returned to his shoulder, and was unconcernedly eating a grape.

"It's Roger!" gasped the Lord Chamberlain.

"Phew! What a relief," agreed Doctor Coldfingers, mopping his brow. "Don't worry, Queen Freda. I'm sure everything will be all right now."

Roger leaned out as far as he could go, and called down.

"Sorry about that, Yer Majesty. Didn't know it were you, see. Never fret, I'll have ye up in a brace o'shakes, and I don't need no sissy ladder neither. Us men o' the sea do it all with ropes. Belay that whimperin', this be easy stuff."

"I'm whimpering because I'm about to fall," explained King Keith urgently. But Roger had disappeared inside the room to do things with ropes.

Below, the watching crowd shouted up encouragement. Percy and Paula had returned. They hadn't been able to find a tablecloth and Cook was too busy to look for one.

"Hold on, Dad! Roger will rescue you!"

"Do be careful, dear. The dog's right below you, and so is the goldfish pond!"

"Hold tight, Daddy! Don't fall!"

"Be brave, Your Majesty! Don't look down!"

Looking down was the last thing King Keith had in mind. He had a shocking head for heights. Grimly he gritted his teeth and tried to pretend that he was dangling only a few inches from the ground, and that the sound he heard wasn't the noise of tearing flag material.

But it didn't work.

"Here we are, matey," said Roger's voice again. He stood by the window holding a lot of rope in his arms.

"Isn't he wonderful?" sighed the Lord Chamberlain, Doctor Coldfingers, Queen Freda, Prince Percy and Princess Paula admiringly. Roger gave them a cheery wave and thumbs up sign. In those few short seconds he had made a stout sling and was lowering it to poor King Keith, who really looked as though he could do with it.

"Steady goes it, Yer Majesty. Step into the sling and I'll haul ye in. Ready?"

Gingerly, King Keith placed a foot on the sling – and up he went, still wrapped in the shredded Jolly Roger, reeled in like a great, silly fish in a net. As he drew abreast of the window, Roger's rough, hairy, tattooed paw reached out and grabbed him. King Keith had never seen a more beautiful hand in his life. Gratefully, he tumbled in through the window. Saved by the flag. And by Roger, of course.

"'Ere. 'Ave a tot o' rum," said Roger
with a chuckle.

"Thanks," said King Keith, sinking into
the hammock. "I don't mind if I do."

He did. It tasted awful. Roger roared
with laughter and slapped him on the
back.

"By the way," said King Keith,
shamefacedly. "I'm afraid I took your
log-book. Here it is. I was going to show it
to everyone. I'm very sorry. I'm sorry
about your flag too. Thank you very much
for rescuing me."

"All in a day's pirating," said Roger with
a wink. "But I accept yer apology. 'Twas
spoken like a true king."

When Queen Freda, Percy, Paula, the
Lord Chamberlain and Doctor Coldfingers
came bursting in a few minutes later, they
were very surprised to find King Keith and
Roger laughing and chatting away as
though they were long lost friends.

The Tide Turns

"I just don't know what got into me," said King Keith to Queen Freda, Percy and Paula as they went down to breakfast the following morning.

"The hall does look nice, doesn't it?" remarked Queen Freda. "Though I say it myself."

"He really is a very decent chap, you know, once you get to know him," continued King Keith. "Knows nothing about gardening, of course, but gave me a lot of useful tips on how to forecast the weather. And what he doesn't know about fishing you could write on a tadpole's tail.

It's rather nice down at the Pig and Slopbucket, Freda, you must come with us sometime."

"We kept telling you how nice he is," said Paula. "It's just that you refused to see his good side."

"I know," admitted King Keith sheepishly. "I suppose I was a bit jealous. He's so jolly, isn't he? Compared to me, I mean. I know I'm a bit stuffy sometimes."

"Oh, Keith," said Queen Freda, giving him a little hug. "You are silly."

Just then, the Lord Chamberlain came hurrying up. Doctor Coldfingers was right behind him. They both looked rather pale and anxious.

"Bad news, I'm afraid," the Lord Chamberlain said gravely. "It's Roger. He's gone."

"What?" came the disbelieving chorus.

"Slipped quietly away to sea during the night," sniffed Doctor Coldfingers. "Only Cook saw him leave."

"Oh dear," said Queen Freda, "what a pity."

"Without even saying goodbye?" wailed Paula.

"But we never made the rum and raisin drink," complained Percy.

"Just as I was getting used to the idea," added King Keith.

"He told Cook it would be better that way. He says he'll miss us all. But he's left presents for us in our rooms. And something for you in the bathroom, Your Majesty," said the Lord Chamberlain to King Keith.

It's amazing how cheerful people get at the thought of a present. Everyone brightened up and hurried off to see what Roger had left for them.

"Oh I say!" exclaimed Doctor

Coldfingers. "A concertina! How ripping!"

"Just what I always wanted," said the Lord Chamberlain, smiling through his tears at the best Ship-In-A-Bottle kit gold could buy.

"Wow!" gasped Paula and Percy. They each had identical huge paper parcels – and inside were complete pirate outfits. Percy's was green and Paula's was blue. Roger had remembered everything, right down to the swords and pistols. And two tiny bottles of rum.

"Best not show Mum," agreed Percy and Paula.

Down in the kitchen, Cook rocked to and fro and cried over a framed photograph of Pamela and a glossy new recipe book called *Twenty Things to do with Salt Fish*.

Queen Freda was standing at her window, trying out her new telescope. On a clear day, you could just about see the sea.

In the bathroom, King Keith stared in amazement at an empty bottle of bubble bath floating amongst soap suds.

"Well I'm darned," he said. "A message in a bottle."

It was. And this is what it said, in Roger's bold black handwriting:

Dear King Keith,

The tide has turned. I can feel it in me bones. I must return to me ship with all haste. Thankee kindly for putting up with me rough sea-faring ways. This has been the best holiday I've ever had. I shall never forget ye all. Any time ye fancy a cruise on Norma, ye know where to come.

Your obedient servant,

Captain Roger Jolly

P.S. Sorry about the talc and bubble bath. I've left ye a few bags of gold to cover the cost. 'Tis only small change to me.

"Well, well, well," said King Keith. "Isn't that nice? Lodgers aren't so bad after all. I really mustn't make these hasty judgements in future."

And he took all his clothes off and climbed into the bath for a long, hot soak.